Robert D. Zabiegel

Twenty-Six Starlings
Will Fly Through Your Mind

TWENTY-SIX STARLINGS WILL FLY THROUGH YOUR MIND

Barbara Wersba

Drawings by

David Palladini

Harper & Row, Publishers

Library of Congress Cataloging in Publication Data
Wersba, Barbara.
  Twenty-six starlings will fly through your mind.

  SUMMARY: *The 26 letters of the alphabet are strung*
together into a myriad of words and images.
    1. English language—Alphabet—Juvenile literature.
[1. Alphabet]   I. Palladini, David.   II. Title.
PE1155.W37   421'.1   77-3811
ISBN *0-06-026376-8*
ISBN *0-06-026377-6 (lib. bdg.)*

Twenty-Six Starlings Will Fly Through Your Mind

It begins where you begin:
a ladder to fables,
an arrow pointing out the stars.
It begins with something to climb on
and ends with a dazzling Z.
It begins with A,
secret and determined.
The guide.

And *B* brings bandits and balloons.
B, with a round belly and sad face,
searching for butterflies.
B, glancing shyly

at C: the moon's cousin.

Emily, twenty-six starlings will fly through your mind
and twenty-six snowflakes will melt on their wings.
Twenty-six dormice will fall fast asleep.
Twenty-six tigers will roar.

D, weaving drummers and dancers and dreams,
is dignified.
D, the hollow man, decorous,
picking daisies for *E*, who is Emily.

Foolish *F*, missing a foot,
comes hopping as though he were welcome,
comes showing off words like
fallow and famish and faun,
comes whispering things like
fandango.

Comes dragging behind him his memories:
old puppets with feathery hair,
wooden dolls and fantastic fedoras.
Forty falcons and one famous flea.

There is magic in mountains,
secret caverns where
dwarves play with gems.
Hidden grottos with walls
of pure crystal,
and fish-pools
of emerald frogs.
Emily, look for them.

Look for the *G*
who comes girlishly laughing,
an old-fashioned *G* wearing
garnets and gauze.
Her garden is trembling
with glowworms.
Her gloves are of lace.

And beyond her an *H*
stands with staunchness,
an *H* made for acrobats' tricks.
An *H* who is hardy and handsome:
the uncle of *I*.

I is pale and discouraged.

She is blown like a match through the world,

like a twig.

She means ME and MYSELF but is never her own.

She takes comfort in infamous dreams.

Now *J*, *K* and *L* appear, dancing a waltz,
whirling themselves into languid lagoons,
into jasmine and kingdoms of jade.
J, *K* and *L* can play silver-stringed harps.
And sometimes, a coconut drum.

Emily, all of the paper dolls rustle to life,
all of the roses take shape in your mind.
Each nodding star has a name and a face.
The desert is swimming in sound.

And sound is an *M* who imitates mice,
who scampers on marmalade hills.
An *M* with small feet and a *V* in his head:
a clown who sips marigold wine.

M who delights in medallions of cheese,
who loves marjoram, mazes and masques.
M who spends time on the merry-go-round,
waving gaily (and cruelly) to *N*.

O rolls into sight like a hoop or a moon,
greatly satisfied, perfectly calm.
She contains all the mysteries
she wants to contain.
She is gracious, and spacious, and cool.

Pouncing *P*, the proud cat,
is sister to *Q*
and they quarrel
through centuries of prose.
Their arguments range
from the price of a pin
to the possible qualms of a quail.

"Quadratics and quoits!"
screams the *Q* in her rage.
"Quell, querulous, quibble and quench!"
"*Palladium*," purrs the proud *P*.
And is gone.

They fade into mist,
into glassy-smooth lakes
where herons stand watching
their prey.
They ripple the waters
making no sound,
and bubble like fish
with small mouths.
Emily, each one is yours.

Yours is the *R* of rhymes, rainbows, and revelations.

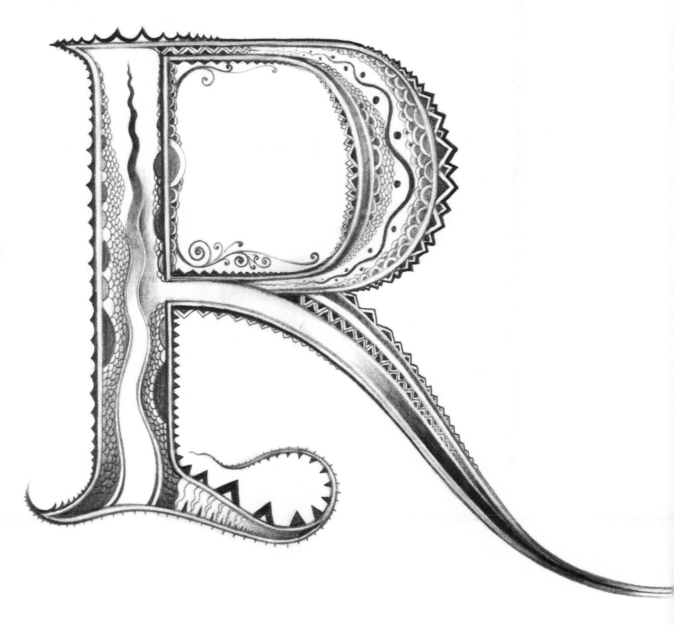

And yours the *S*,
who comes spinning spangles
and sarabands.
S, the good letter,
curved like a prayer,
bringing silver and silence.

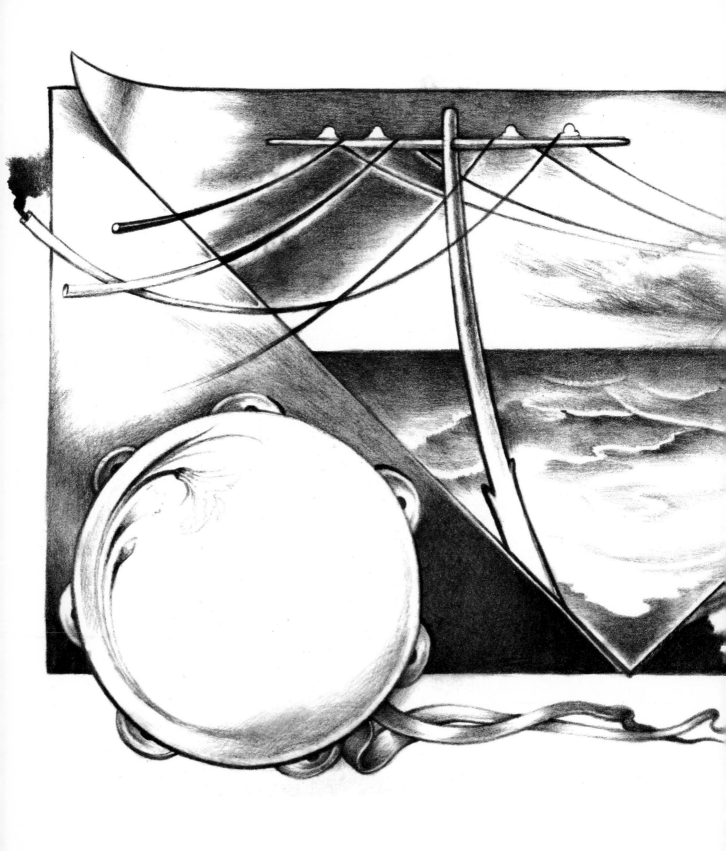

T, with arms outstretched,
stands lonely
on all the beaches
of the world:
waiting for telegrams.

Give him a tambourine,
a trumpet and a timpani.
Let him make music
for the tide.

And music for *U*,
who sees the Universe.
Great *U*, whose mind
can hold a star
within a star,
a flower
in a flower,
and a snowflake
in itself.
Unbounded *U*,
roaming the fields
of space.

V follows him: pointed yet shy.

V who was once in love with *A* and stood on her head.

V, the impossible valentine, writing veiled verses, vacuous odes.

W wanders the woodlands.
He thinks that whimsey and wantonness
take the same path.
He thinks that walruses
sing in their sleep.
He loves weevils and wallabies,
whippoorwills, whispering worms.

And *X* is a crossroad
where unicorns stand,
their horns made of glass.

And Y is a magic tree.
Her apples fall
slowly.

And *Z* is the zigzag
of lightning:
a diamond cracking the sky.
As blossoms whirl upward
and butterflies
turn into gold.
As dolphins sing chanties
for mermaids
with ebony eyes.

Emily, twenty-six starlings
will fly through your mind,
and twenty-six snowflakes
will melt on their wings.

Twenty-six dormice
will fall fast asleep.

Twenty-six tigers will roar.